MIRROR
MAGIC

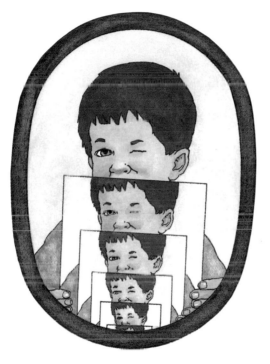

by SEYMOUR SIMON
Illustrated by Anni Matsick

BELL BOOKS

Published by Bell Books
Boyds Mills Press, Inc.
A Highlights Company
910 Church Street
Honesdale, Pennsylvania 18431
Originally published by Lothrop, Lee & Shepard
Publisher Cataloging-in-Publication Data
Simon, Seymour.
  Mirror magic/by Seymour Simon; illustrated by Anni Matsick.
  48 p.: col. ill.; cm.
  Includes index.
Summary: Explains how mirrors work and presents activities to illustrate the
scientific principles involved. Experiments for young children are included.
ISBN 1-878093-07-X
1. Mirrors—Juvenile Literature. 2. Science—Experiments—Juvenile Literature.
[1. Mirrors. 2. Science—Experiments.] I. Matsick, Anni. II. Title.
 535/.323-dc20   1991
LC Card Number 90-85921
Distributed by St. Martin's Press
Printed in the United States of America

For Joyce and her magic mirror
                    S.S.

For Amos
        A.M.

Did you wash your face this morning? How did you know that it was clean? Did you have to ask someone? Or did you just take a look at yourself in a mirror?

5

Have you ever wondered why you can see yourself in a mirror? Mirrors are made of smooth, polished surfaces. The surfaces reflect light and send back an image of things. Like a ball, light bounces away from an object it hits. Mirrors make an image because they bounce back light in a way called **regular reflection**.

7

Then why isn't the wall in your room or a page in this book like a mirror? It's because the wall or the page is not really smooth. Touch the wall and the page with your fingertips. You can feel that they are rougher than the surface of a glass mirror.

When light hits a rough surface, it bounces off in many directions. The light is scattered and so is the image. Otherwise, you might see your image on this page instead of print.

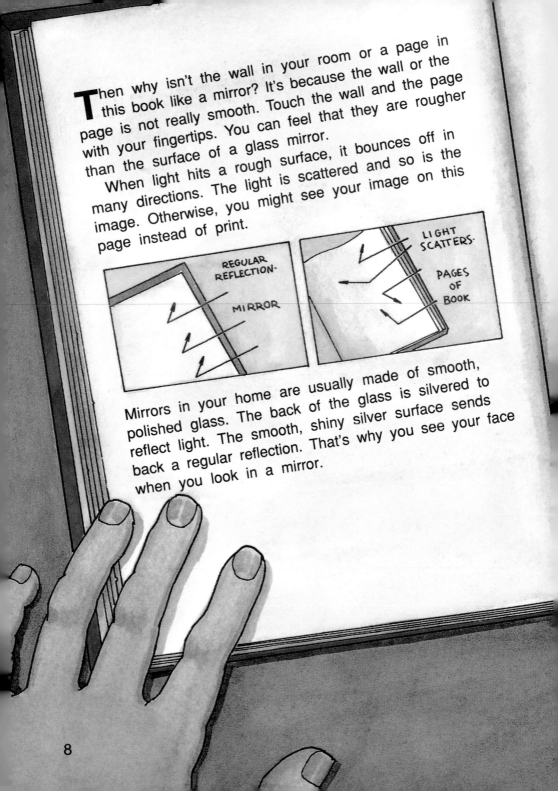

REGULAR REFLECTION.

MIRROR

LIGHT SCATTERS.

PAGES OF BOOK

Mirrors in your home are usually made of smooth, polished glass. The back of the glass is silvered to reflect light. The smooth, shiny silver surface sends back a regular reflection. That's why you see your face when you look in a mirror.

Are you and your mirror image exactly alike? Are you sure? Here's a simple way to find out. Look in a mirror and cover your right eye with your hand. What do you see?

Ask a friend to stand alongside your mirror image, facing you, and cover her right eye with her hand. Compare your mirror image with the sight of your friend. Does it look as if the same eye is covered?

A mirror reverses your image. When you see yourself in a mirror, the image is not quite the same as the way your friends see you.

What do you see when you hold these sentences in front of a mirror?

Hold me up
to a mirror

You can read the first sentence because the mirror has turned it around (reversed it). What happens to the second sentence when you look at it in the mirror?

Hold me up
to a
mirror

Of course, you've seen yourself in a mirror many times. You've become very used to your mirror image. So you can easily comb your hair or adjust your clothing while looking at your image. But can you make a simple drawing while looking in a mirror? It might be harder than you think.

Stand a small mirror on a sheet of plain paper. Place a book behind the mirror as a support. Draw a square and a circle on the paper.

Then hold your nondrawing hand between your eyes and the paper. Adjust your hand so that you can see the paper and your hand in the mirror but not directly. With your drawing hand, try to trace the drawings as you look at their images in the mirror.

Most people find that this isn't as simple as they think. Your hand doesn't seem to go the way you expect. You seem to have little control over the direction your hand is moving. It's a strange feeling.

Try signing your name as you watch your hand in the mirror. Try writing a sentence. Do you have any problems in writing when you look in a mirror? It's easy to become mixed up.

As you draw or write, the mirror reverses your view, so the signals sent to your brain are reversed. You can learn how to draw and write while looking in a mirror, but it takes lots of practice.

One famous person wrote all his notebooks in a "secret" backward mirror writing. They became readable only when held up to a mirror. This great scientist and artist lived in Italy five hundred years ago. His name was Leonardo da Vinci.

Now you can understand why looking at a mirror image is not exactly the same as looking directly at an object. But you *can* use mirrors to see yourself in the same way that others see you. Here's how.

You will need two small mirrors and some tape. Hinge the mirrors together with the tape. Stand the hinged mirrors side by side on a table so that they form an "L" shape. Now look at yourself in the middle where the mirrors meet. You may have to change the angle of the mirrors slightly to get your image to be correct.

Cover your right eye with your right hand. What happens to your image? What happens when you turn your head to the left? Hold the sentences on pages 12 and 13 in front of the hinged mirrors. How do they look now? Try combing your hair while looking at your image. Do you have any difficulty?

You can see a correct image of yourself in the corner of the two mirrors. That's because you are looking at a mirror image of another mirror image. Your image is reversed twice. When you reverse something twice, it looks the way it did at first.

21

Here's how you can use the same hinged mirrors to see more than one image of an object. Place a toy inside the angle made by the hinged mirrors. How many images can you see in the mirrors? Does each image look the same?

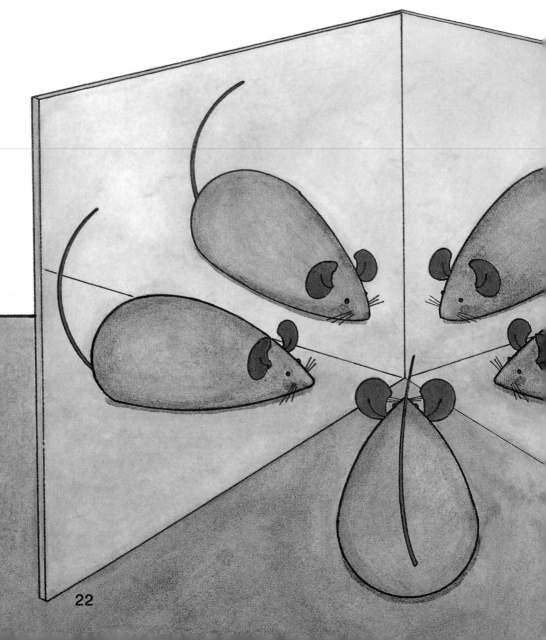

22

Watch how the images increase in number as you slowly bring the mirrors together. Each of the images changes as you move the mirrors. The number of images depends not only on the angle of the mirrors, but also on the position of the toy and your eyes.

For another bit of mirror magic, you will need a third mirror. Place the third mirror flat on a table and stand the hinged mirrors on it side by side. Open the hinged mirrors so they form an "L" shape. The three mirrors now form a **corner cube mirror.**

Look at your image in the corner where all three mirrors come together. No matter how you move, your image is always reflected right back to you.

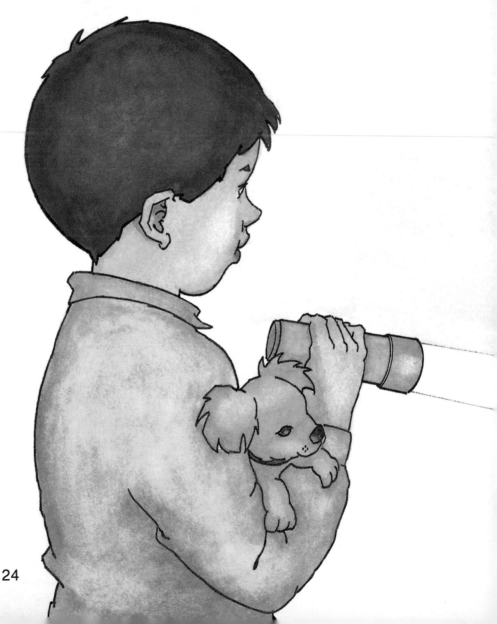

24

Try shining a flashlight beam into the corner. The light beam is reflected straight back to the flashlight no matter what direction it comes from. The reflectors on bicycles or automobiles are made of glass or plastic in the shape of many small corner cube mirrors. They help drivers to see bikes or cars at night.

Here's a way to see many images of yourself at the same time. Stand in front of a large mirror and hold a smaller mirror facing the larger one. Look into the smaller mirror, twisting it slightly until you see one image of yourself after another in the larger mirror. How many can you see? Is each image the same? Close your right eye. What happens in each image?

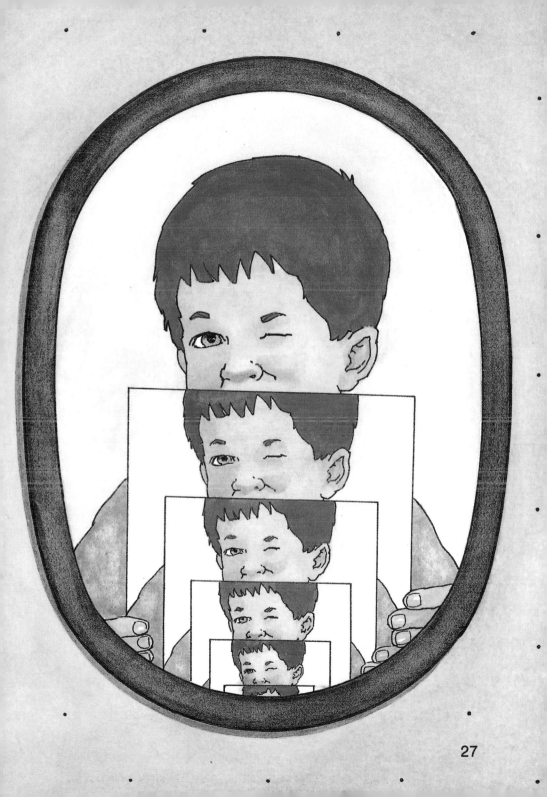

Mirrors can show you things that are usually difficult to see. Turn your back to a large mirror. Hold a small mirror in front of you and slightly to one side of your face. Look into the small mirror and you can see the back of your head.

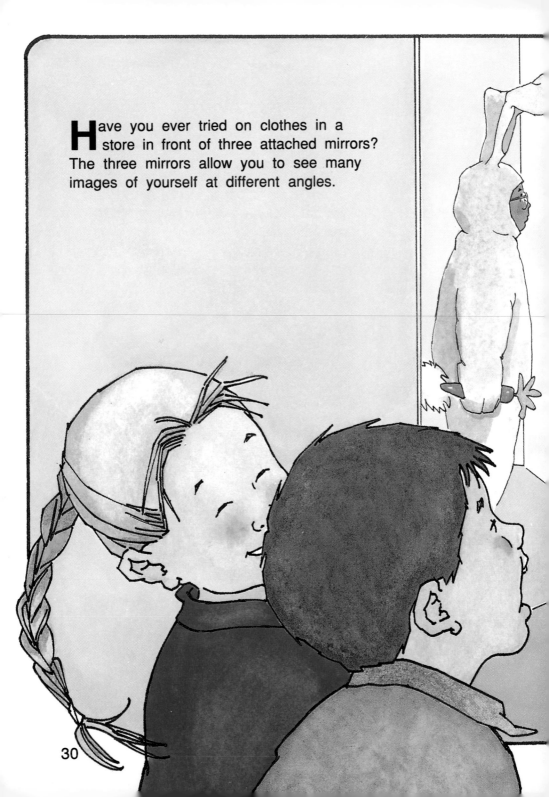

Have you ever tried on clothes in a store in front of three attached mirrors? The three mirrors allow you to see many images of yourself at different angles.

30

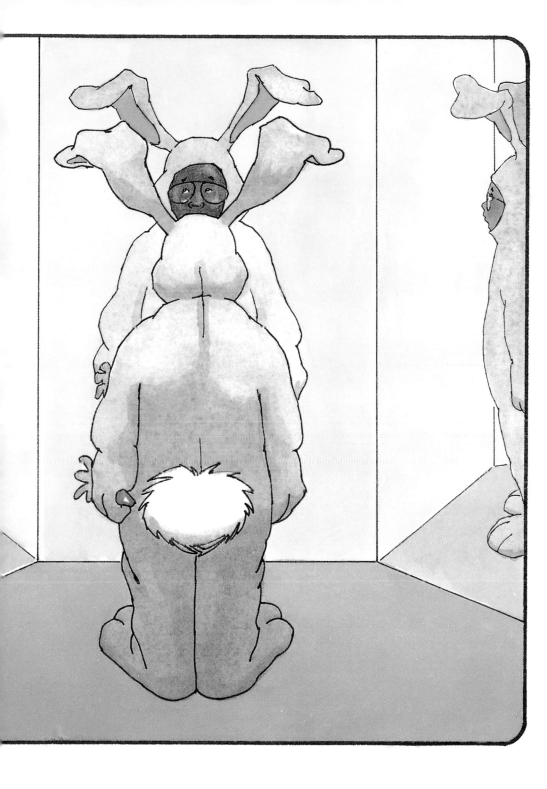

You can use a mirror to look behind you without turning your head. Automobile drivers use little rearview mirrors for that purpose all the time. They help make automobile driving much safer. How could a rearview mirror make bicycle riding safer?

PALOS EAST MEDIA CENTER
7700 W. 127th St.
Palos Heights, IL 60463

Would you like to use a mirror to see around corners? Place a mirror at an angle outside the door of a room. You can see what's going on down the hall. Sometimes, at a sharp bend of a road or a parking ramp, there is a mirror mounted in such a way that it lets a driver see if a car is coming from the other direction.

Here's how to make a special instrument that lets you see around corners or over high walls. You will need two small mirrors, tape, scissors, and a long box such as a shoe box.

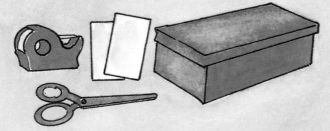

Tape the mirrors across the corners at each end of the box as shown in the drawing. Cut two holes in the top of the box directly above the mirrors. Tape the box closed. You have made an instrument called a **periscope.**

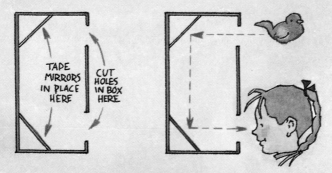

TAPE MIRRORS IN PLACE HERE

CUT HOLES IN BOX HERE

Submarines use periscopes. They are long tubes that are raised when the submarine is just below the waves. Through them, people in the submarine can see what is happening on the surface of the water. Can you think of any other ways to use a periscope?

37

Have you ever seen yourself in the special mirrors at an amusement park? Some mirrors make you look short and fat. Other mirrors make you look long and thin. Still others make you look fat in the middle and thin on top and bottom.

Fun house mirrors are different from ordinary mirrors. Remember that an ordinary mirror is made of flat glass. The mirrors in a fun house are curved in different ways. A curved mirror will change an image to make it large or small or a mixture of different shapes.

Some bathroom mirrors are curved, so that when you look in them your image is enlarged. Even if you don't have an enlarging mirror, you have other curved mirrors in your house. You may not think of them as mirrors, but they are.

A shiny soupspoon is a mirror. Hold one in front of you and you can see some funny faces. Now turn the spoon over and look at the back to see some different funny faces.

How does your image in a spoon differ from your image in a flat mirror? What happens to your image when you hold the spoon sideways or at an angle?

You can use mirrors to make pretty patterns of light and color. Here's how. You will need three small mirrors all the same size and shape, some tape, a rubber band, a piece of waxed paper, and some small pieces of different-colored papers. Tape the mirrors together as shown in the drawing. Cover the bottom with the waxed paper fastened with the rubber band. Drop a few pieces of colored paper into the opening at the top. Holding the mirrors upright over a light or a white surface, look through the top of the taped-together mirrors. You will see six-sided patterns of color. You have made an instrument called a **kaleidoscope.**

Shake the kaleidoscope slightly while you look into it. The patterns will change into other shapes and designs. A kaleidoscope reflects images over and over again to make an ever-changing display. For other patterns, just replace the pieces of paper with new ones of different shapes and colors.

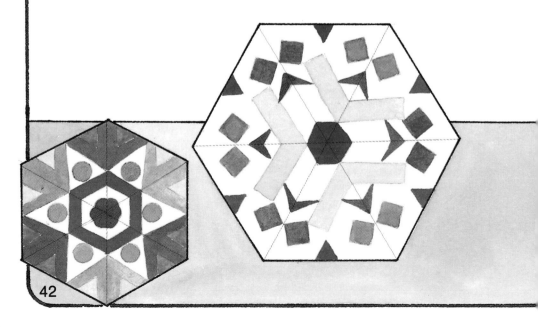

42

People use mirrors for all kinds of reasons. Astronomers use large, curved mirrors in telescopes to gather light from distant stars. Dentists use little mirrors to look into people's mouths. Doctors examine people with instruments that have mirrors. Barbers show people their new haircuts with mirrors. Magicians use mirrors to make things appear and disappear.

How many mirrors do you have in your house? How many ways can you think of to use them? Just look in one of your mirrors and reflect . . .

INDEX

535.3
SIM

COPY **2**

Simon, Seymour

Mirror magic

DATE DUE

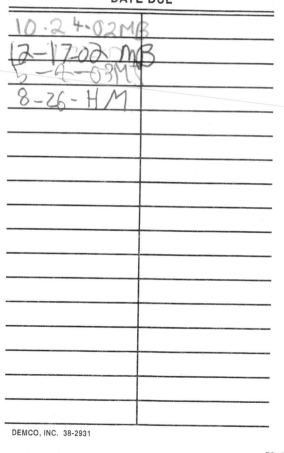

10·2 4·02MB	
12-17-02 MB	
5-4-03M	
8-26- HM	